# Eddie and Fred

## WE'RE ALL HEROES

Written By

**Andrea Perez** and **Diana Reynolds**

To our little heroes
# Kayla, Maya, Jack, Troy and Aria

Published in association with Bear With Us Productions

©2021 Andrea Perez and Diana Reynolds
The rights of Andrea Perez and Diana Reynolds as the authors of this work has been asserted by their accordance with the Copyright Designs and Patents Act 1988.

Library of Congress Control Number: 2021906649

Written By
**Andrea Perez** and **Diana Reynolds**

Eddie and Fred
WE'RE ALL HEROES

Illustrated By
**Caner Soylu**

Eddie and Fred make such a great pair,
best friends forever,
always showing they care.
They play, they laugh,
they have a good time,
no better friends you ever will find.

Fred is a hero in his dreams at night,

a legend, an idol, showing his might.

**"Ta da! I'm here! I'll save the day!**

**Watch out, you bad guys – get out of my way!"**

Fred zooms around with a mask and a cape,
flying down stairs and not taking a break.

He trips,
 he twirls,
  he lands with a

crash!

Then Eddie darts
over as quick as a

FLASH!

"Hey, are you hurt?" Eddie dusts Fred off.
"No, I'm okay," he replies with a cough.
"I just want to be what I see in my dreams,
flying so high, a hero supreme.

want to be brave
nd to stand up so tall,
ut it's hard when I try,
nd I tend to fall.
My legs are too short
nd my ears are too long,
even with four legs, I'm
ust not that strong!"

"You have confused what **a hero really means**,
it's not only the characters you watch on the screen.
**A hero doesn't need a cape or a mask,**
**you're better** than Batman, Thor and the Flash.

Super powers come **from deep within**,
not measured by race or your color of skin.
**A hero doesn't need to be strong and tall;**
they can be **any shape, big or small."**

"What kind of powers come **from the heart?**
Let's **take a moment to think**, and then start.
There are so **many traits** that we can possess,
when we use **the right powers, we'll be a success!**

Let's take a walk; **we'll spot heroes in town.**
No need to read comics, they live all around!
**They're normal people**, like you and me.
We'll go outside and then you will see."

**"KINDNESS** is where I would like to begin.
**Being kind to others is always a win.**
**Show love** to those less fortunate than you;
a smile, a hug or **a helping hand** will do."

Fred sees a girl, sad and alone.
**"I'll ask her to play
so she's not on her own.**

It's good **to be kind;**
it's the right thing to do,
and others will show
kindness right back to you!"

"Next we have **COURAGE** to help your friends.
If you see bullying, **stop and defend.**
Take a deep breath, **be confident and strong,**
explain what they're doing simply is wrong!"

"There!" calls out Fred. "They are starting a fight!
I'll go and tell them that **fighting's not right.**
It hurts, it's wrong, it **makes you feel sad.**
We **must show** the bullies what they're doing is bad."

"Fred, you're **so brave,** you are doing what's right.
You **used your words** and did not join the fight.

Let go of your fear and **stand up tall,**
　　　If you need more help, **give a grown-up a call."**

"Last but not least we bring you **FRIENDSHIP.**
This is **a power** we surely can't skip!
Friendship involves most powers combined,
use all of **your qualities** and a friend you will find.

To be a good friend you need **love in your heart.**
Be **trustworthy and fair** and share from the start.
Be quick to **say sorry** and share how you feel.
This way your friendship is **stronger and real."**

**"A friend will accept you for just who you are.**
They **won't try to change you,** they'll think you're a star!

They'll keep all your secrets and be **someone you trust.**
**Supporting** each other is simply a must."

"Fred, our friendship's **as strong as they come.**

Of all of my buddies, **you're number one!**

You **listen,** you **care,**
you're **honest** and **true.**

But all of this
**you already knew."**

**"We are all heroes!** Now I can see
a hero is already inside you and me.
**Be a good friend, courageous and kind,**
**a hero** in yourself is what **you will find."**

The **END**

# About **the Authors**

Andrea and Diana are sisters, best friends and now co-authors of their first children's book. Andrea, mom of two, is an elementary school counselor in New York. After publishing her memoir, she discovered her love for writing children's books and partnered up with her sister Diana to write Eddie and Fred: We're All Heroes. Diana, mom of three, loves teaching core values to her kids through books and life situations. Together their hope is to spread kindness and love of reading to all through the real-life characters, Eddie and Fred.

**www.AndreaPerez.net**

Made in the USA
Columbia, SC
30 November 2022